GATHER UP, GATHER IN

A Book of Seasons

By M.C. HELLDORFER · Illustrated by JUDY PEDERSEN

PUFFIN BOOKS

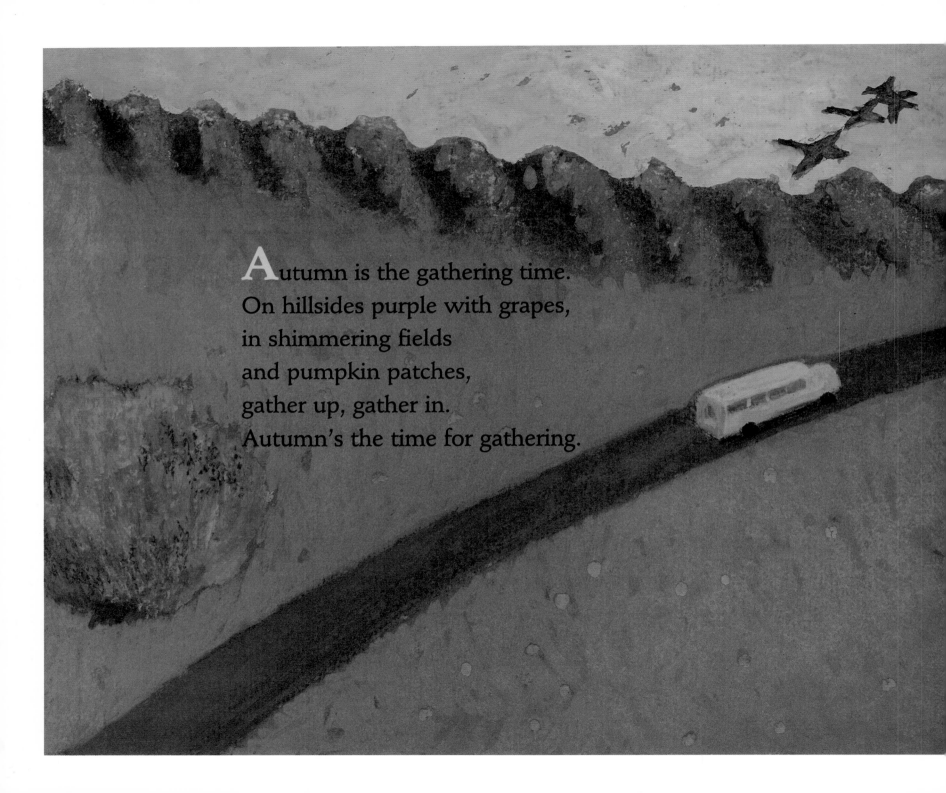

Autumn is the gathering time.
On hillsides purple with grapes,
in shimmering fields
and pumpkin patches,
gather up, gather in.
Autumn's the time for gathering.

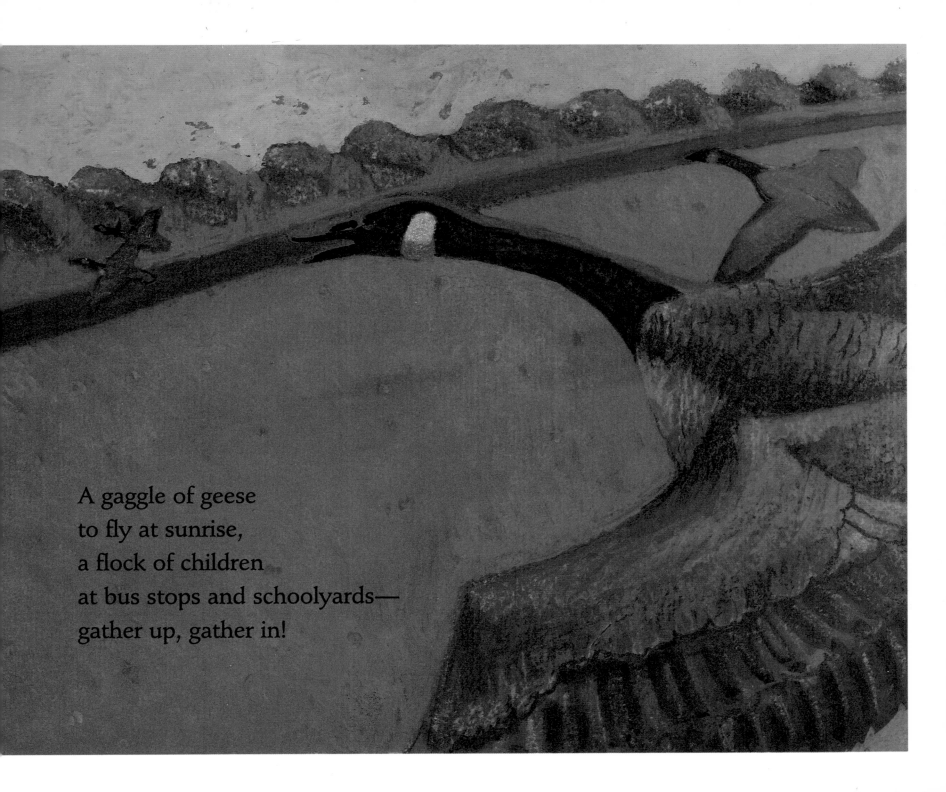

A gaggle of geese
to fly at sunrise,
a flock of children
at bus stops and schoolyards—
gather up, gather in!

Autumn's the time for gathering
wood for fires,
seeds for spring,
leaves, and wind, and leaves again.
Gather up, gather in.
Mice steal cheese,
squirrels find nuts.
Autumn's the time for gathering.

One misty night
spooks appear,
door to door
gathering treats.
Then just like that
they're gone.

Just like that
the trees are bare.
The geese have flown,
and children are home by fires.
The grapes are jam,
and pumpkins, pie.

Gather up, gather in,
gather close tonight:
Winter slips in.

Winter slips in quietly,
wisping fences white with snow,
erasing sidewalks, disguising trees,
burying toys, keeping lost keys
secret beneath the snow.

It writes a code on icy windows.
Inside we whisper and tie a bow
around a box, then tuck our secret
underneath the stair. Shh—
Winter keeps secrets everywhere!

In crusty snow, where feet write riddles:
paw prints, boot prints, little steps, leaps!
Who went where, then who went there?
But Winter keeps these secrets secret.

In trees, where squirrels open up
their secret cupboards of nuts;
in caves, where soft-breathed bears
dream secret honey dreams;
under the bridge, where a nest of mice
sleeps hidden beneath its cap of snow,
where children skate on moon-white ice,
while fish swim secret paths below.

Winter is so deep in secrets
March won't tell what it knows—
what is hidden beneath soft snows—
But *I* know this secret secret:

Spring.

There is no stopping Spring
from spilling down the mountainsides,
washing valleys with snowy tides,
and splashing yards with flowers.

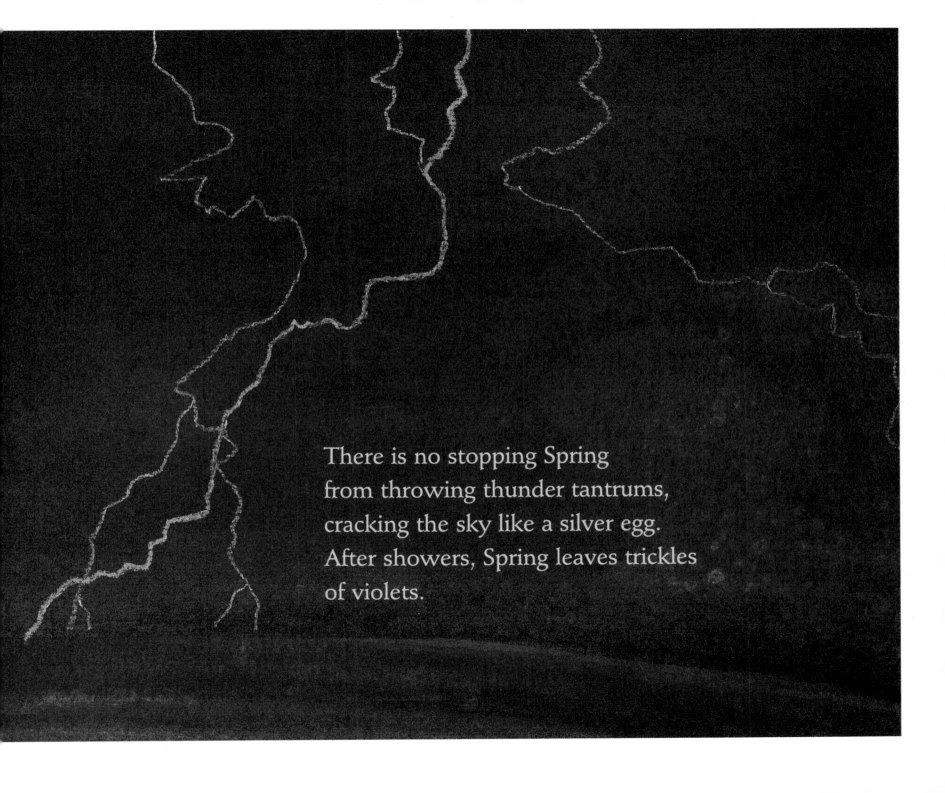

There is no stopping Spring
from throwing thunder tantrums,
cracking the sky like a silver egg.
After showers, Spring leaves trickles
of violets.

We spring out of doors,
toes popping through old tennis shoes,
wrists poking out of sleeves,
our legs too long for last year's pants—
for there is no stopping Spring!

When seeds blow like shining wishes,
and children wind-spin across the park,
when birds, like bottles of quivery song,
uncork all at once,
when trees shake down pink confetti
and laughter floats through open windows
and notes spill out of Mr. Ragogini's piano,
who can stop Spring?

None, I think,
but Summer.

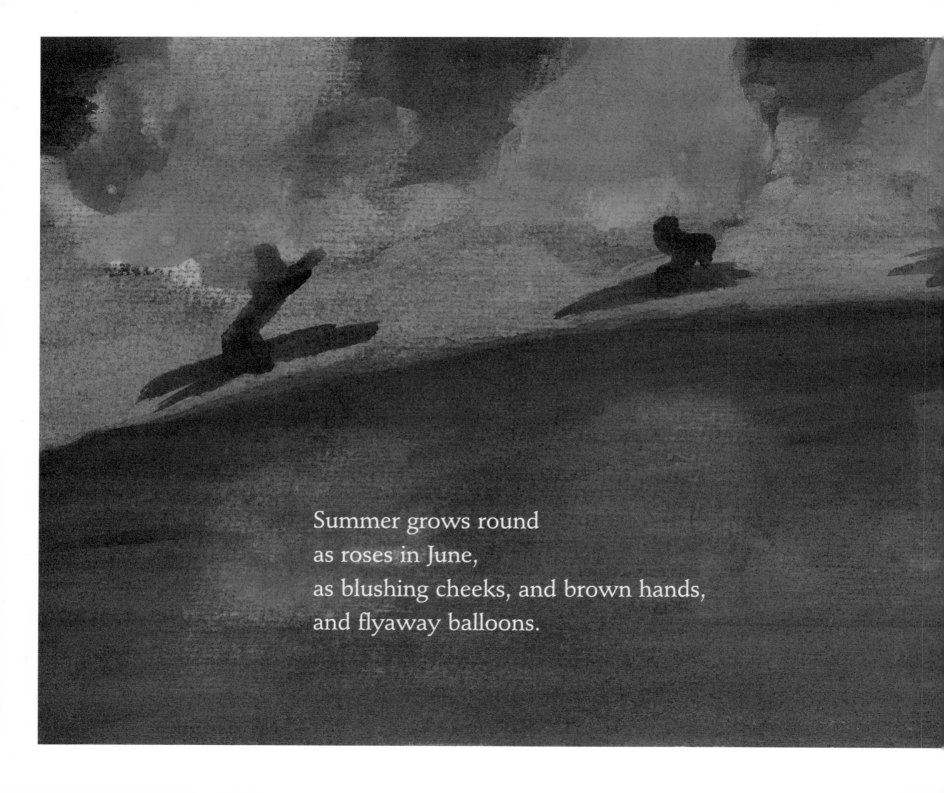

Summer grows round
as roses in June,
as blushing cheeks, and brown hands,
and flyaway balloons.

Roll down a hill,
and summer turns around you.
Roll over waves
and summer swirls around you.

Twirl under a water sprinkler,
wrap yourself inside a rainbow,
and dance round and round
till the trees spin,
and the leaves turn,
and one leaf twirls
down.

See Summer spin away.
Autumn comes round.

For Bob
in all seasons
—M. C. H.

For Amanda and Matthew
—J. P.

PUFFIN BOOKS
Published by the Penguin Group
Penguin Putnam Inc., 375 Hudson Street, New York, New York 10014, U.S.A.
Penguin Books Ltd, 27 Wrights Lane, London W8 5TZ, England
Penguin Books Australia Ltd, Ringwood, Victoria, Australia
Penguin Books Canada Ltd, 10 Alcorn Avenue, Toronto, Ontario, Canada M4V 3B2
Penguin Books (N.Z.) Ltd, 182-190 Wairau Road, Auckland 10, New Zealand

Penguin Books Ltd, Registered Offices: Harmondsworth, Middlesex, England

First published in the United States of America by Viking,
a division of Penguin Books USA Inc., 1994
Published in Puffin Books, 1998

1 3 5 7 9 10 8 6 4 2

THE LIBRARY OF CONGRESS HAS CATALOGED THE VIKING EDITION AS FOLLOWS:
Helldorfer, Mary-Claire.
Gather up, gather in : a book of seasons / by M. C. Helldorfer ;
illustrated by Judy Pedersen. p. cm.
Summary: Words and pictures evoke the changing seasons.
ISBN 0-670-84752-6
[1. Seasons—Fiction.] I. Pedersen, Judy, ill. II. Title.
PZ7.H37418Gat 1994 [E]—dc20 94-9148 CIP AC

Puffin Books ISBN 0-14-054847-5

Printed in the United States of America